The Stone Street

A Flashback *story set in*
Roman Britain AD *410*

For Rose Stirling

The
Stone Street

Marilyn Tolhurst

Illustrated by Alan Fraser

A & C Black · London

FLASHBACKS

Julie and the Queen of Tonga · Rachel Anderson
Across the Roman Wall · Theresa Breslin
The Doctor's Daughter · Norma Clarke
A Candle in the Dark · Adèle Geras
All the Gold in the World · Robert Leeson
Casting the Gods Adrift · Geraldine McCaughrean
The Saga of Aslak · Susan Price
A Ghost-Light in the Attic · Pat Thomson
Mission to Marathon · Geoffrey Trease

First paperback edition 1998
First published 1998 in hardback by
A & C Black (Publishers) Ltd
35 Bedford Row, London WC1R 4JH

Text copyright © 1998 Marilyn Tolhurst
Illustrations copyright © 1998 Alan Fraser

ISBN 0-7136-4727-2

Photoset in 12/19 Linotron Palatino.

Printed in Great Britain by St Edmundsbury Press Ltd,
Bury St Edmunds, Suffolk

Contents

Glossary 6

What happened at the beginning 7

Map: Roman Britannia AD 410 8

1 The Villa Deserted 9

2 Ickinos 21

3 The Smith's Boy 33

4 The Fen Road 44

5 The Saltings 53

6 The Black Causeway 64

7 The Sacrifice 72

8 The Stone Street 79

But what happened after? 87

Further Reading 88

Glossary

Aquitania A region of southwest France.

atrium The open main courtyard of a Roman house on to which most rooms led.

centurion Roman army officer in charge of a century, a unit of 100 men; later, the number of men in a unit was reduced to 80.

coracle Small, roundish boat made of water-proofed hides stretched over a wicker frame.

fen Low-lying, flat marshland.

Gaul France.

legion A unit of the Roman army, the size of which varied throughout history. At the time of this story a legion may have contained as many as 5,000 men.

optio Second in command to the **centurion**.

palisade A strong fence made of stakes driven into the ground, especially for defence.

praetorium The house of a commanding officer.

triclinium Dining room.

trivet A three-legged metal stand on which cooking vessels are supported over a fire.

wold A tract of open, rolling countryside.

What happened at the beginning

In the spring of the year AD 410, on the night before his sudden departure, Old Lupus buried his gold. Not all of it, not by any means. The coin he took with him – as much as he could carry. But the golden jewellery and the decorated spoons and the heavy silver dishes he buried in a wooden casket in the fields beyond the Villa Ursini. He paced out the spot carefully from the edge of the ditch to the great oak tree by the track, for Old Lupus intended to come back for his treasure as soon as the danger was over. But he never did return. And as chance would have it, no one discovered his gold for over a thousand years. But that's another story. On the night he buried it, someone saw his shadow slinking out into the fields carrying the great casket before him. When he returned in the thin light of dawn his hands were empty.

*

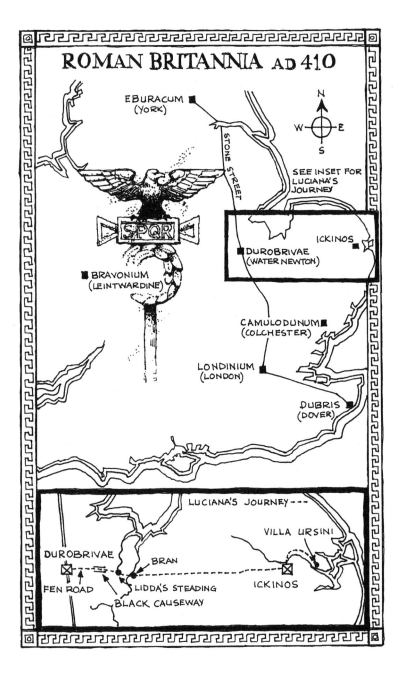

ROMAN BRITANNIA AD 410

EBURACUM
(YORK)

STONE STREET

N
W — E
S

SEE INSET FOR
LUCIANA'S
JOURNEY

SPQR

ICKINOS

DUROBRIVAE
(WATER NEWTON)

■ BRAVONIUM
(LEINTWARDINE)

CAMULODUNUM
(COLCHESTER)

LONDINIUM
(LONDON)

DUBRIS
(DOVER)

LUCIANA'S JOURNEY - - -

VILLA URSINI

DUROBRIVAE

BRAN

FEN ROAD

LIDDA'S STEADING

BLACK CAUSEWAY

ICKINOS

· 1 ·

The Villa Deserted

It was the black dog Ferox who woke her. He growled deep in his throat and Luciana started up in fear. No one slept easy in their beds those nights for every spring tide brought the fear of raiders from the sea, men with yellow hair and great swords of iron who thieved and burned and killed. For many nights the beacons had blazed from headland to headland warning of their approach. So far, the Villa Ursini had escaped their swift and savage raids but no one believed that it would be for long.

Luciana, in her little room above the atrium, placed a warning hand on the dog's neck as she peered through a hole in the shutters.

'Hush Ferox, it's only Uncle Lupus. I think he is getting ready to leave.'

She lay back in the darkness, cradling the dog against her for warmth. Fear gripped her with icy fingers. Everyone was leaving. Her aunt, the lady Agrippa, had already gone, taking with her only two slaves and her son Titus the halfwit. The villa servants had melted away to their villages taking whatever they could carry. The peasants had ransacked the outhouses, the cattle had mysteriously disappeared from the fields, even the dovecote was empty. Only Old Lupus remained with his body slave Cassio, and he was now pacing the villa with a restless tread.

Quintus Maximus Lupus, the name suited him well, for Lupus meant wolf and he was yellow-eyed and yellow-fanged with a temper as sour as crab apples. Tax-gatherer and moneylender, he was lord of the great Villa Ursini and many wide acres beyond. His wealth was a legend. It was rumoured that he held lands in Aquitania and some said, even in Rome itself. But the Emperor saw little of the taxes that Old Lupus gathered in his name and the payments brought no relief to the people of this forgotten quarter of Britannia. Luciana had heard it whispered that there were many among the local population who would have slit his throat for the price of his silken toga. It was only a matter of time before he too disappeared.

Luciana shivered in her narrow bed. Soon there would be no one left in the villa but herself and

Ferox. What then? She thought of the scavenging Saxons who harried the coast night after night, rowing silently up the reedy estuaries to plunder and burn. Any night now they might come.

'Where is my father?' she whimpered into Ferox's fur. But Marius Maximus was far away in Eburacum. Her last sight of him had been months before when he had ridden away to join his legion, his armour newly oiled, his crested helmet gleaming in the sun.

It did not surprise her that she had been forgotten; she had never been wanted in the Villa Ursini. With her mother dead and her father away, she had always been treated like a slave. She had spent most of her childhood running errands around the villa for Aunt Agrippa. Luciana screwed up her face in fury. Her aunt, a vain and silly woman, had once cut off Luciana's long red hair to have it made into a hairpiece for herself. Old Lupus was no better. He looked on her with hate in his yellow eyes, perhaps because she was sound of limb and quick-witted, unlike his only son Titus who was crooked from birth and simple in his ways.

Titus. Luciana sighed when she thought of his clouded blue eyes and his high-pitched laugh. He had been her constant companion from childhood and his absence made her heart ache. She wondered how he would fare on his mother's estate in Gaul. For that was where he had gone and where Old Lupus would go, too, now that it had become so dangerous to stay.

'Just the two of us now,' Luciana whispered in the dog's ear. She spoke as if he understood her, as well he might for his brown eyes were bright with knowing. She had found him, newly whelped, in a ditch by the black fen three years before. Abandoned by his mother, his little body had struggled for life and she had taken pity on him, thinking that she herself might have suffered the same fate if her uncle had had his way. She sneaked him into the villa wrapped in a blanket and fed him on drops of milk and honey until he could manage scraps from the kitchen. Then he had grown strong and swift, his rough coat black and curly, a cunning hunter and a devoted friend.

Ferox licked her face and smiled his doggy smile. She smiled back trying to quell the fear that snagged at her breath and made her hands feel cold and clammy.

'We must leave too, Ferox, as soon as it is light. We will gather what we can and make our way to Ickinos. Perhaps Cato will know where my father is.'

She crept downstairs in the early light of morning to find the villa hearth-cold and deserted. The rooms echoed with eerie emptiness as she moved through them. Nearly everything had gone – the furniture, the cushions, the fine plate, even the pots and pans by the brazier in the kitchen. Awed by the silence, she fought to hold down the panic that rose in her throat as she looked about her. She had spent all of her thirteen years in the villa, she knew every room and corridor. It had been built centuries before when the Roman Empire was young and since then it had been patched up and renewed many times. It was old and dilapidated but never had it been so silent. Luciana crept around it searching for signs of life. But in all the ranges of outbuildings, the bathhouses, the court-yards and the maze of corridors, nothing stirred. Even the birds were silent.

In the triclinium where the family dined, Luciana stopped to look at the painted walls. From faded portraits, eyes stared back at her with expressions of blank indifference. Views of fine gardens with grape vines and olive trees bloomed on the plaster. Many times she had made up stories about the pictures to tell Titus. Neither of them had ever seen a real olive tree and for a second she wondered if Titus had gone to a place where they grew. Under her feet the elaborate mosaic floor was cold and dull with dust. She had often swept and beeswaxed it on the occasions when Old Lupus held a banquet. Then it shone in the lamplight with glowing patterns of red and ochre, its scenes of gods and goddesses almost leaping from the floor.

Slowly, as if sleepwalking, Luciana made her way to the kitchens. Ferox padded silently behind her. She pushed open the door of a dark storeroom and knelt on the floor, feeling for a loose tile in the corner. Squeezing her fingers between the cracks she heaved it up to reveal a rectangular hole beneath. She had dug out the hole years before when she had been locked in the room as a punishment. It was her secret place. In it she had hidden everything she owned and valued. Feeling inside it with a trembling hand she now withdrew a small bundle and a leather pouch. The bundle contained her doll Flora, made for her one winter by the old ploughman who lived above the barn. It was of jointed wood with a painted face and plaited yellow wool for hair. She had spent many happy evenings sewing little clothes for it. She laid it down tenderly and turned her attention to the leather pouch, emptying its contents into the palm of her hand.

Five gold coins glimmered in the half-light. Solidi. Each one bore the head of the Emperor Constantine and each one represented a visit from her father. Five times she had seen him over the years and each time he had given her gold. It was her own personal fortune. She fingered each of the coins in turn. She loved them not for what

they could buy but because they were gifts from him. She was half afraid to carry them because someone might try to steal them from her.

But there was one more thing in the secret place, more precious than the rest. It was her father's last gift, a bracelet made specially for her. She unwrapped it carefully from its piece of silken cloth and gazed down at it. Made of pierced gold, it was intricately patterned with a clasp in the form of a snake. Around it in golden letters were the words *UTERE FELIX LUCIANA* (*Wear it, lucky Luciana*).

Her eyes filled with tears as she looked at it. She had always kept the bracelet hidden for fear that Old Lupus would take it away, and now she could not wear it. Of all the days of her life, this was the surely the unhappiest. She stowed it away in the leather pouch with the coins and, taking a deep breath to steady herself, rose to her feet and tied the pouch to her belt.

Ferox, who had been nosing around the store-room, had found an old bone and was cracking it noisily with his strong white teeth but when Luciana called to him he picked it up obediently and followed her. By the villa entrance she stopped by a recess cut into the wall. Inside it stood the statue of Vesta, goddess of the hearth. She had been there as long as the villa and Luciana had always loved her quiet face. It was no longer the custom to offer her daily gifts of wine and flowers for the villa now had a Christian temple in the grounds. But no one was rash enough to dispose of one of the household gods, however ancient, so Vesta remained in her shrine accepting whatever small honours came her way.

Today, Luciana stopped before her and thought that it must be the first time, in all her long years there, that Vesta had presided over an empty villa. For a second her mind conjured up a picture of the sea raiders breaking in and smashing the statue against the wall. Reaching out, she picked up the little figure and carried her back to the storeroom by the kitchen. Kneeling on the floor she made a little whispered speech.

'When I am gone, Lady of the Hearth, the villa will be empty and it may be a long time before anyone comes here in peace. I leave you here for safety. To you I dedicate my doll Flora who will keep you company and I make an offering of gold. Grant me luck on my journey and, and—'

Luciana's words failed her as she tried to imagine her future. 'And a hearth to warm myself at.' Thoughts of her father and Titus filled her mind as she whispered one last urgent wish. 'And please, oh please, let me find those I love.'

Her heart choked with misery, she laid Vesta in the secret place under the floor with Flora beside her and one of her precious gold coins between them. Then she replaced the tile. Ferox stood by, his bone between his front paws, seeming to understand the solemnity of the moment.

Luciana stood up and brushed the dirt from her hands and knees. 'Come Ferox,' she said with sudden determination. 'We must gather what we can find for our journey.

She ransacked the villa for anything useful that had been left. There was not much to eat and she found only a stale flat loaf, the last of a sack of dried peas and some withered yellow apples in the barn loft. She bundled these into a length of linen cloth which she tied to a stick so that she could carry it over her shoulder. Her best find was a small iron knife that had been left behind in the kitchen. She fingered its blade grimly before tucking it into her belt. In her room she picked over her meagre collection of clothes, selecting a coarse linen tunic and a thick woollen cloak with a hood for the journey. For once, she was grateful that Old Lupus had never allowed her to wear fine sandals; her sturdy footwear with thick studded soles was just the thing for a long walk.

Pulling on her cloak and shouldering her pack, she whistled Ferox to follow and stepped out into the bright spring morning. A mixture of fear and excitement tingled through her veins. As she passed under the arched gateway she glanced up at the carved faces of Janus, god of the doorway, whose image crested the arch. With his double profile that looked both ways, he was also the god of journeys. Luciana bowed to him gravely before she set off on the track towards Ickinos.

On the crest of the hill she took one last look back at the villa nestling in the valley below her. A shaft of early morning sunlight caught its flint walls and red-tiled roof, making it blaze with colour for an instant.

'Farewell home,' said Luciana softly, tears blurring her vision.

As Ferox bounded joyfully ahead, she turned her face to the road.

· 2 ·

Ickinos

Following the course of the river, Luciana made her way towards the town of Ickinos. It was a journey she had made often before, either on errands for Aunt Agrippa to the goldsmith's or the cloth importer's, or to take Titus to his lessons with Cato. At the thought of Titus her eyes again filled with tears. He had never been a willing schoolboy and would always linger on the way, preferring to throw stones in the river or pick berries along the path. It was she who had been the apt pupil, enjoying scratching her letters into the wax tablet and learning to recite poetry. Once, she had made the mistake of showing Aunt Agrippa how she had written her name in ink on a scrap of papyrus. Her aunt had slapped her and said that she did not pay Cato good money for educating slaves.

Today, frightened and heartsore, the journey seemed longer than ever. She skirted a village at the bend in the river, keeping hold of Ferox's collar as the village dogs set up a fearsome barking. A ragged child emerged at the edge of the palisade and threw stones at them, making her feel more lonely and unwanted than ever. Cato was her only hope. Of all the people in the world, after her father and Titus, he was the one she loved and trusted most. He was a Greek, one of many who made a living as clerks and teachers to the Roman legions. Cato had served twenty-five years with the Sixth Victrix and had been a close friend of her father. Now, he lived in retirement in Ickinos working as a teacher and letter writer to the people of the town.

Luciana walked fast, pausing only to eat an apple and a crust of bread on the way. The path was bright with early blossom and Ferox bounded happily in and out of the bushes sniffing at rat holes in the bank and chasing moorhens into the water. Finally, turning a bend, she came in sight of the town and paused for breath, looking at it. Ickinos. Its earthen banks, topped with great walls of flint, reared up before her. Massive drum towers bulged along its length and native huts clung to its flanks like burs. In the still morning air hundreds of plumes of smoke drifted upwards from cooking fires and braziers.

The old town was still busy, even though river trade had dwindled because of pirates in the eastern sea. Today, there were no merchant ships at the mooring although the great river gate stood open for trade. Nervously, Luciana made her way towards it. The gateway swarmed with soldiers. They were not the legionaries of Rome but hired men, foreigners, who fought for whoever paid them most. One of them, a great bearded man in a leather tunic, barred her way with a spear and said something to her in a language she could not understand.

Ferox growled ominously and the soldier aimed a kick at him. Luciana suddenly ducked under his arm and dashed into the street with Ferox streaking behind her. She heard laughter from the gate and knew that the soldier had only meant to frighten her.

She scurried towards Cato's house with her heart beating uncomfortably fast. The alleys were slippery with garbage and slops and she had to dodge past carts and dirty children playing in the gutters. In the forum she stopped to catch her breath. The buildings were shabby, showing only a trace of their former glory. The public fountain, once such a feature of the square, was broken, its basin green with moss. A few traders had set up stalls but their goods were poor and highly priced. Under the colonnades, men clustered around the taverns and cookshops exchanging news of the latest raids. Luciana skirted round them cautiously and made her way to Cato's apartment. He lived above a pastry cook's shop in a suite of comfortable and well-furnished rooms. Diving up the dark stairwell with Ferox at her heel, she banged urgently on the heavy oak door.

It creaked open on its iron hinges to reveal

Livia, Cato's domestic slave. She looked down in some surprise at the pinched white face of the girl standing on the step.

'I must see Cato,' Luciana blurted out. 'Please let me see him, it's important.'

Cato must have heard her for he appeared in the vestibule and greeted her with a smile. Tall and olive-skinned with heavy black brows, he looked fierce to those who did not know him.

'Luciana, my dear, what brings you into Ickinos today?' He led her into the room that served as his study. Ferox padded in silently behind them and stretched out on the cool floor beneath the table.

The sight of a sympathetic face was suddenly too much and Luciana found herself weeping uncontrollably as she tried to find words.

'They've gone,' she finally managed to say between sobs. 'Everyone. Old Lupus left last night. And the villa is bare. Not a thing left – nothing. I don't know what to do.'

Cato gathered her against his toga and stroked her shoulder. His face was grave. 'They've left you all alone?'

He called out to Livia, 'Some wine please and something to eat for Luciana.'

He sat her down on one of the couches in the room and eventually coaxed a full explanation from her. Then he sat in his teacher's chair and lapsed into deep thought.

'It does not surprise me that Old Lupus is gone,' he said at length. 'In times like these a rich old rogue like him is never safe. But to leave you alone when you were under his care—' He shook his head in disbelief. 'Not that he will find safety elsewhere. The Emperor Honorius himself is under threat. He sits snug enough in his palace in Ravenna but the barbarians are advancing from the north. Soon they will rattle the very gates of Rome.'

He reached across to a scroll that lay on his desk and unrolled it slowly, casting his eyes over the script.

'I have had news today from the garrison at Camulodunum. The legions are being withdrawn from Britannia.'

Luciana gasped.

'The Empire cracks before our very eyes. The Emperor is recalling the outlying legions to protect its heart.' Cato's solemn brown eyes bored into Luciana's white face. 'We live at the outer edge of civilisation. I fear we will be cast into darkness.'

Luciana's mouth was suddenly dry, her eyes wide with fear. 'But what of my father? What of Marius? Will he go too?'

'The message has gone to the Victrix in Eburacum. They will be preparing to march even as I speak.'

Luciana buried her face in her hands. Finding her father had been her great golden hope. To have that snatched away from her now was more than she could bear.

'I will go to him,' she said desperately. 'I will find him. Maybe he will take me with him.'

Cato got up and clasped her hands in his. 'That is foolish Luciana. You must be brave, like all of us. You can stay here with me in Ickinos. You are a good scholar. I will make you my clerk and you will help me. Heaven only knows, the skills of civilisation will be sorely needed when the barbarians come.'

'No,' said Luciana, her face white and set. 'Thank you, Cato, you are kind to me and I honour you for it but I must find my father. I could not bear it if he left without me, without seeing me.'

Cato clicked his tongue. 'Be sensible, Luciana. The legion will march down the Stone Street to the port of Dubris. The only way to intercept them would be to cross the great fen to the fort at Durobrivae. It is a desolate road with danger on every hand. A fully-armed man would quail to walk that way alone.'

'I have Ferox,' said Luciana stoutly. 'He will protect me.'

Cato's tone became sharper. 'The people of the fenlands are little more than savages,' he said impatiently. 'They will rob you, and sell you into slavery – maybe worse. They ambush travellers from hidden places in the reeds. And the villages are like island fortresses bristling with spears. In places the road is nothing more than a crooked thread across a sea of black mud. You could drown – or die of the marsh fever.'

There was a silence that Cato took for assent. Livia entered the room with a tray containing sweet wine and some honey cakes from the cook-shop below. Cato poured some wine into little silver drinking cups and handed one to Luciana.

'Good Gaulish wine,' he said. 'Maybe the last we shall see. Drink it up. Soon we shall have to get used to drinking ale like barbarians.'

Ferox thrust his nose into Luciana's lap. She

stroked it absently and offered him crumbs from her honey cake.

For a while she and Cato spoke of other things but later, as she stood by the open shutters looking down at the street below, she made up her mind.

'Cato,' she began, turning to him and picking her words carefully. 'I thank you for your advice. I understand that the fen road is dangerous but I must try to reach my father. I should never forgive myself if I didn't. Ickinos itself may fall to the raiders, so to stay or to go is equally risky. I have some gold – coins my father gave me. I will buy some supplies and take my chance. If I set off for Durobrivae tomorrow, I may at least see the legion as it passes on its way.'

Cato opened his mouth as if to argue but then spread his hands in a gesture of acceptance. 'I have said my words of warning, Luciana. If you must go, then you must. I will give you what help I can. See here.' He reached for a large wax tablet, one of those he used for his teaching, and poised himself above it, stylus in hand.

'Imagine you are a bird in flight, Luciana, looking down at the country below. You would see the coast here.' He drew a curving line in the wax.

'And Ickinos here.' He drew a small rectangle. 'If you were flying very high you would see Eburacum here . . . Londinium here . . . and the port of Dubris here. The legion will march this way. If you crossed the great fen to the fort at Durobrivae you might meet them on the Stone Street.'

'How far is it?' asked Luciana, looking at the map.

'Seven days march. Maybe more. The way is slow and you will need to carry supplies. There are rivers to cross, you will need money for a ferry-man and maybe bribes for the hunting people who live by the Black Causeway.' He looked up at her. 'Can you do this, just a girl and a dog?'

'I can do it,' said Luciana tightening her jaw. 'With the help of the gods.'

Cato sat back looking at her. 'Then we must equip you,' he said simply.

They spent the rest of the afternoon making preparations, buying food, extra clothing and useful supplies. Cato packed it all in an old leather knapsack that he had used when he was a legionary. Luciana tested it for weight. It was heavy but not impossible.

After dinner which was taken in the Roman manner,

reclining on couches around a small low table, Cato lit the oil lamps and sat down at his desk. 'I will write down everything I know of the fen road,' he said. 'I have never travelled it myself but I have often sent legion messengers that way. There are villas along the route here and there where you might find a welcome and there are places where you must take great care. I will also write a letter to the garrison commander at Durobrivae telling him of your business. It will get you entry to the fort. While I do this Luciana, you must sew your gold coins into the hem of your tunic. They are worth a great deal and must only be used in dire need.'

He summoned Livia to supply a needle and thread. Then in the soft silence of the lamplit room he scratched away with his stylus while Luciana sewed her precious gold into its new hiding place. When she had finished, she took her golden bracelet and clasped it around her arm above the elbow, hidden by her clothes. The feel of the cold metal against her skin was reassuring and she felt in her heart that it would bring her luck.

On the floor at her feet Ferox dozed, happily chasing hares in his sleep, unaware of the great adventure that lay ahead.

· 3 ·

The Smith's Boy

She set off at first light the following morning. Livia pressed upon her a parcel of dried fish, smoked meat and a wheaten loaf to eat on the journey. Cato accompanied her as far as the West Gate. The great doors were still locked and barred but the smaller gate for foot passengers stood open with a sentry standing by.

Luciana put up her hood against the fresh morning air and adjusted the straps of her pack. Cato handed her a little leather purse.

'Small coins,' he said. 'In case you should need them. Save your gold for later.' He shook his head regretfully. 'If I were a younger man, I'd come with you. But I fear my marching days are done. Remember me to Marius when you find him. And send me word when you are safe.'

They embraced and Luciana saw tears shining in his eyes as they parted.

'Keep the setting sun before you,' he called as she turned to wave.

As she set off, Luciana felt a thrill of excitement, mingled with fear about the journey ahead. But it felt good to be doing something rather than waiting, always waiting. The morning was bright but chilly, and the ground was dry underfoot. The road was wide and straight with a bank and ditch on either side, its surface rutted by cart wheels. At the first milestone she looked back for the last time at the town of Ickinos. Its towers looked strong enough. She made a brief wish that Cato would be safe.

All morning she walked at a steady pace. As yet there was no sign of the fenland with its sinking mud and warlike villages. The countryside was fertile and well-tilled, divided into neat fields. On the way she passed peasants going to market and traders with strings of pack ponies. Once, she saw a chariot speeding into Ickinos with the government mail. No one took any notice of the girl and her dog tramping along the edge of the road.

At midday, hot and footsore, she stopped by the side of a wood to rest and eat Livia's picnic. She shared the food equally with Ferox who bolted it down in seconds and then ran off to investigate further supplies in the bushes. Luciana took off her sandals and lay with her head on her pack, looking up at the sky between the pattern of oak leaves above. Thoughts of her childhood in the villa floated across her mind like clouds as she drifted off to sleep.

How much time elapsed she did not know but she woke suddenly to find a face peering down at her. It was a boy's face, nut brown and dirty from the dust of the road, framed by a mop of fairish hair. Luciana started up in alarm and she saw a sudden grin pass over his face.

'Thought you were dead,' he said, leaning back on his stick and adding conversationally, 'I found a dead man by the road once – I took his pack.'

Luciana scrambled to her feet. Her heart was thumping wildly. He was not much older than she was but he had a dangerous, knowing look about him. Scrawny, dressed in a ragged tunic and a matted goatskin jerkin, he held the rein of a pack pony that grazed quietly by the wayside as he spoke.

'You don't often see girls on the road,' he said, eyes narrowing in speculation. 'Lost your parents?'

Luciana was silent and he grinned again. 'Lost your tongue as well?'

She responded suddenly in a tone that would have done credit to Aunt Agrippa. 'I'm on my way to join my father in Durobrivae, not that it's any of your business.'

The boy gave a low whistle. 'That's six, seven days from here, across the fen. They eat people alive down there.'

He laughed as Luciana flinched and drew back. Ferox reappeared at her side and growled. But the boy whistled again, a low soft whistle between his teeth, and Ferox quietened and allowed his muzzle to be stroked.

'Good dog,' said the boy soothingly. 'Good hunting dog.'

Luciana glanced at the pack pony. It was well-laden with equipment and there were weapons too. She could see the handles of knives sticking out from the canvas panniers and there was a light bow strung across the pack-saddle.

'I see you're a traveller,' she said severely. 'A tinker. We used to get them at the villa sometimes, asking to mend the pots and pans. They were always stealing things.'

The boy scowled at her. 'Not a tinker,' he said ferociously. 'A smith. My father was the best bronzesmith this side of the Stone Street. He could make anything, mend anything – a horse harness, weapons, fine jewellery for fat Roman ladies.' His face twisted in a sneer. 'We never stole anything.'

'Except dead men's packs,' countered Luciana with spirit.

'That was fair,' said the boy. 'He wasn't going to need it.'

'Where's your father now?' asked Luciana, looking around her.

'Dead,' said the boy shortly. 'Marsh fever. I'm

working the roads alone now.' He pulled on the reins of his pony. 'I don't fancy your chances going west,' he said contemptuously. 'Not if the salt-workers find you. They'll make a slave of you soon as look at you, a fine Roman girl like you with snotty manners.' He spat on the ground. 'You're lucky I didn't rob you myself.'

He turned to go, snapping the pony's leading rein with a vicious crack. Luciana pulled her cloak tightly round herself. In spite of the midday sun she felt cold and wished she had not insulted him. It seemed like a bad omen.

All afternoon she trudged westwards following the tracks of the smith's boy. Sometimes she glimpsed him ahead and sometimes she saw his footprints in the dust. She was bone-tired and her shoulders ached from the pack. As dusk began to gather she knew she must look for a safe place to spend the night. Ferox, tireless in his adventures, suddenly sprinted across an open field and returned with a dead hare in his mouth. Luciana wrestled it from him, tied its legs with twine and suspended it from her pack. It would make a meal for them both later.

Fear crept up on her again at the thought of spending the night in the wild. Cato had shown her how to make a rough tent from a strip of canvas tied to a tree and pegged to the ground, the way legionaries did on the march. He had given her a spool of twine, and a flint and steel for making fire. She found a clearing in a small thicket and put down her pack with a sigh.

'This is *my* camp,' said a sharp voice from behind her.

Spinning round she saw the smith's boy and his pony in a secluded spot out of sight of the road. She was about to make an angry reply when she checked herself. Instead, holding out the dead hare, she said, 'If you will share your camp, we will share our supper.'

After a short silence he accepted her offer with a nod and told her to collect wood for a fire. Then he set about unsaddling the pony.

Luciana gathered an armful of sticks and watched as he struck sparks with his strike-a-light on to scraps of tinder which he blew up to a flame. Soon they had a crackling fire and she set about skinning the hare. Darkness crept up on them and owls began to hoot; in the distance a wolf howled.

She shivered and looked up at the huge velvet sky and the rising moon. This was the first night she had spent without a roof over her head.

The smith's boy hobbled the pony to stop it straying in the night and fed it some oats from a sack. Then, when the fire was glowing and the ash was hot, he put the hare on a spit and placed it over the fire supported by crooked sticks. Luciana set some apples to bake. As the smell of their supper scented the air, she realised how hungry she was.

His name was Vennorix. He did not know how old he was and he could neither read nor write but, as he told Luciana, he knew how to work bronze and how to survive on the road. Not that he said very much to her and he certainly did not ask her name.

They ate the meat off the bone with a loaf of bread and washed it down with some weak ale that he had in a leather flask. The scraps and bones were tossed to Ferox. Mellowed by the meal, Vennorix took up a hazel stick and whittled at it idly with his knife. He seemed a little more ready for conversation so Luciana told him how she had been abandoned in the villa and of her plans to

intercept the Sixth Victrix on the Stone Street. He nodded slightly, his eyes watching her narrowly.

'And you?' she asked when she had finished her story. 'Where are you bound?'

'West,' he said. 'Beyond the Stone Street. Trade's no good here. The harvest was bad last year and half the villages are starving. There's talk of plague in Camulodunum and the Saxon men are raiding all down the coast.'

'Are you going to the fort at Durobrivae?' asked Luciana

'Maybe.' He paused in his carving and looked up at her.

'Can I journey with you?' she asked.

'No.'

There was a silence in which Luciana felt a surge of anger. She considered offering him money to be her escort as far as the fort but then she thought he might rob her and leave her destitute. The silence grew longer and finally he broke it.

'I travel alone. It's best that way. I come and go as I please and no one notices me. I don't want to look after a girl who can't look after herself. What use would you be to me?'

· 4 ·

The Fen Road

Luciana woke at dawn, stiff and cold, covered lightly in dew despite her makeshift awning. The night had been full of terrors – nightmares and the distant baying of wolves. Ferox had slept fitfully against her, occasionally lifting his head to sniff the night air.

She rose painfully and stretched her limbs. The smith's boy was already up and was blowing on the embers of the fire. He did not speak but handed her half a loaf of barley bread and threw down some scraps for Ferox. Luciana shook out her cloak and warmed her hands at the fire. She gazed into it bleakly, unable to find words to express her thoughts.

Eventually, having eaten, she rolled up her canvas cover and gathered her pack. Cold fear had settled in the pit of her stomach and for a moment she thought of pleading with him to let her accompany him on the journey. But pride prevented her and courage forced her steps towards the track. Looking back in a wordless farewell she caught his eye for a moment. He grinned up at her. 'Don't stray from the road Roman girl. Soon you'll meet the fen where the ground will swallow you up if you let it. By and by you'll come to a broad river. Ask for Bran the coracle maker and he'll row you across. Tell him Vennorix sends his greetings.'

As she set off, the sun rose above the horizon, sending her shadow leaping ahead. Emerging from the wood she came to an open wold of ragged turf dotted with golden gorse bushes. As she swung along the track she tried to quell her fears about the possible dangers ahead.

Suddenly, as the land dipped away to the west, she saw it – the great fen. Flat as a table top and boundless as the sea, it stretched away from her until it blended in a blue mist with the sky. Below her at the edge of the wold lay the firm fen, bright green and dotted with mares and their colts. Beyond that was the brown peat, the deep fen with here and there a dark clump of alder trees rising above it. And in the distance, hazy in the morning sunlight, lay great beds of emerald-coloured reed and shining expanses of water teeming with flocks of wildfowl.

Luciana drew in her breath as she gazed down at this unknown watery landscape. 'Keep to the road,' she repeated to herself. 'Keep to the road or the ground will swallow you.' She pulled up her hood and trudged on, singing snatches of childhood songs to keep her spirits up. The road as yet was broad and high, zigzagging slightly to keep to the firmer ground but safe enough. For miles she passed no one and stopped only once to rest and eat in a sunny spot under a willow. Solitude settled on her like a second cloak, the silence broken only by birdsong and the sound of the wind rustling in the reeds.

When the sun was high she finally came in sight of human habitation. On a spur of higher ground, clusters of low straggling buildings raised themselves above the reed beds. Swine and geese dotted the rough pasture. Ahead of her she could see the broad river that Vennorix had mentioned. Labourers in the fields watched her with curious eyes but no one offered a greeting. At the river's edge the road ended in a rough wooden jetty and she stood for a moment looking across the wide expanse of wind-ruffled water.

Beyond it the reed beds looked thick and darkly impenetrable.

The noise of hammering caught her attention and she turned towards a wooden hut roofed in turf. It was surrounded by nets, eel traps and racks for drying fish. Gathering her courage she peered into the dim, fish-smelling interior to where a man was working.

'I am looking for Bran the coracle maker.' Her voice, even in her own ears sounded reedy and tense, the accent too Romanised. The man glanced up.

'And what do you want with him?'

He wore a greasy tunic and plaid leggings. His arms, bare to the elbow, were covered in tattooed spirals. Fierce blue eyes stared at her from a leathery face, weighing her up, taking in her fine wool cloak, her sturdy sandals and her pack. Luciana held on to Ferox's collar and said, 'I bring greetings from Vennorix, the smith's boy, and a request that Bran the coracle maker might row me across the river.'

He stood up, brushing his hands. 'I am Bran the coracle maker. And I can row you across the river – for a fee. But the country is wet and wild there my lady. Ask yourself if you really need to go that way, for it is best avoided if you travel alone.'

'I have business in Durobrivae,' said Luciana. 'And if that is the road, then I must take it.'

He nodded, not taking his eyes from her face. 'And where is the boy Vennorix?'

'He . . . he also travels alone. He will come this way later, perhaps.'

Bran laughed. 'No, not this way. He will take the hidden way across the dark fen to the fording place where his pony may cross. He is an artful boy, not always to be trusted, but skilled in many things. He goes his own route to the saltings yonder. Now let me see the colour of your money.'

Luciana felt for her purse and pulled out a silver denarius. She saw Bran's eyes gleam and she knew she was offering too much but she proffered it anyway and he accepted it without comment.

The leathern coracle seemed as flimsy as an eggshell as he lowered it into the water and Luciana feared for her life as she stepped in. Ferox had to be persuaded into her arms and he fretted and whined as Bran rowed them into midstream.

The current was strong and he pulled far into it before allowing the run of the river to wash them down to the opposite shore. The wind had risen a little as she stepped out, and the prospect ahead looked bleak.

Bran watched her without expression. 'When the way divides, take the right-hand path. By nightfall you will come to the place of Lidda the salt trader. He might give you shelter.' He pushed the coracle back into the river. 'But then again, he might not. Good luck, my lady.'

The way was long and hazardous. Luciana toiled along, hemmed in by swaying reeds and with mud sucking at her ankles. Wildfowl sprang up in raucous commotion at almost every step, sending Ferox into a constant frenzy of chasing. As the sun began to dip she longed for a sight of Lidda's homestead however dangerous it might be. The thought of spending a night under this limitless sky caused her stomach to cramp with fear. Then, at a place where the path divided, she saw the pony. It stood patiently by the track tethered to an alder tree. Above it, seated on a branch and half hidden by the foliage, sat Vennorix.

A flood of relief swept over her as if she had seen a long lost relative. He swung his legs idly and whistled to Ferox.

'So far, so good, Roman girl,' he said as he jumped down. 'You've made good time. Your little Roman feet must be raw.'

Luciana managed a grin. 'I am footsore, tinker, but still walking.'

'The saltings are down yonder,' he said, pointing. 'I can get you lodgings for the night – if you will pay me.'

'What if I have no money?'

'Then you sleep under the stars. Come, a coin or two will do it. I will tell Lidda you are an orphan and I am taking you to the slave market in Durobrivae. He won't argue. He might even want to buy you himself.'

'I'm no slave!' cried Luciana hotly.

'No, but you could be – all too easily.' He gave a nasty leer and held out his palm. 'Some silver, Roman girl, and you have my protection.'

Luciana drew herself up. 'If I am alive and free in the morning, tinker, I shall reward you. But not till then.'

· 5 ·

The Saltings

Lidda's settlement clustered untidily on a spur of land overlooking a wide tidal creek. Protected by the fen on one side and open water on the other, it was a little island kingdom in the lonely landscape. On the landward side it was ringed by a palisade of fearsomely spiked wood. Vennorix beat on the gate with his stick and shouted a greeting as they were admitted to a teeming yard full of strutting geese and chickens. Two rangy hounds sprang at them with bared teeth and there was a great commotion as Luciana tried to restrain Ferox.

Suddenly, a tall figure emerged from a thatched roundhouse and strode towards them, dispatching the snarling dogs with a kick. He was a brawny man of thirty or more with long plaited hair and a fine tunic of saffron yellow. His bare arms were banded with golden armrings and there was a drop of crystal hanging from one ear. His outlandish appearance caused Luciana to shrink back and pull her cloak around her. But on seeing the smith's boy, the man's face broke into a broad smile.

'Vennorix!' He clapped the boy on both shoulders. 'You're welcome and more. We have need of your skills here. How goes life on the road?'

Vennorix shrugged and pulled a face. 'Well enough, if you take no heed of plague and famine. And with you Lidda?'

Lidda laughed. 'We don't grow fat on our profits, that is certain. But people still need to salt their broth. Come, stable your pony and we will talk awhile.'

His eyes took in Luciana and narrowed in speculation. 'You have a companion, Venn. A wife?' He grinned. 'Or a captive, maybe?'

'Na, na.' Vennorix spat in an unconcerned manner. 'An orphan I picked up on the road. I am taking her to Durobrivae, to find her a place . . . you know.' He winked at Lidda who laughed back. 'She'll fetch a good price, I'm thinking.'

Luciana stared at them with fury shining in her eyes but she said nothing. She followed them to the roundhouse where she crept into the shadows and sat down with Ferox against her.

It was a large space with low benches set around a smouldering peat fire. Barley cakes were baking on hot stones around the hearth and a cauldron of meat stew hung on a chain over the embers. The aromatic smell of peat smoke and cooking made her feel tired and hungry at the same time. A woman came in with a jug of ale and soon Lidda and Vennorix were deep in conversation.

Drowsily, Luciana heard them discussing trade and politics, raids and skirmishes. Her ears pricked up when she heard Vennorix say, 'Now that the legions are ordered back to Rome, there are soldiers deserting everywhere. The roads are full of them. Most of them were born here and see no reason to risk their lives for the Emperor. Many are heading west. There is an old centurion, out Bravonium way, who is making up a fighting force to keep the Saxon dogs out. That's where I'm bound. Where there's an army, there's always need of a smith.'

The woman came back again and ladled the stew into wooden bowls. After serving the men she handed Luciana a bowl and a hunk of barley bread. There was no spoon but it did not matter, she was so hungry that she polished off the meal in minutes. There was a heap of sheepskins by one of the benches, evil-smelling but invitingly soft. She crept up against them and was soon in a deep dreamless sleep.

She was awoken by a kick in the ribs. Daylight was filtering through the chinks in the walls and Vennorix stood above her.

'Well, it's morning Roman girl, and you're still alive and free.'

She ignored him and got up. 'When are we

leaving, tinker? I must be on my way soon. You shall have silver when you get me to the Stone Street.'

'Then you must wait awhile,' he said. 'I have business here – and you can make yourself useful.'

He had already set up his forge in a corner of the yard. Grumpily, Luciana dowsed her face in a barrel of water and then went outside to watch. It was a fine day with a soft breeze blowing off the fen. The wide sweep of the river glowed like pearl in the morning light and she could see all the salt trenches at the edge of the water. Vennorix told her that it was the beginning of the salting season. He showed her how the high tides were allowed to sluice into the salt trenches so that some of the water would be evaporated by the sun and wind.

'They boil off the rest of the water in these troughs so that only the salt crystals remain,' he said. 'I am mending all the tools today, just like my father did each year at this time. You are my slave, Roman girl, so you can pump the bellows.'

Luciana scowled, but they worked side by side all day and in spite of herself Luciana became absorbed by the process. Hour after hour she laboured at the sheepskin bellows to keep the heart of the forge fire roaring from red to gold to

fiercely white. Vennorix melted down scraps of old bronze to a brilliantly glowing liquid that he poured into moulds to create new knife blades and ladles and bridle bits. He hammered and riveted and ground new edges for blades, working always with rapt concentration and skill. Finally, when all the work was done and they were both smoke-blackened and smeared with ash, he sat back on his heels and looked at the array of mended tools with satisfaction. 'You're worth your broth tonight my slave. If you're lucky, I might even keep you.'

For an answer, Luciana gave him a sharp push that sent him reeling backwards.

At supper that night, the whole village crowded into Lidda's roundhouse to eat and gossip. It was a strange gathering, quite unlike anything she had ever experienced in the Villa Ursini. Those of rank sat closest to the fire and ale cups made of horn were passed freely amongst them. Luciana sat quietly behind Vennorix, saying nothing but listening carefully. When the talk turned to trade she saw Lidda's face become grave.

'The Venonii west of here are starving,' he said.

'They have great bands of warriors guarding the Black Causeway and extorting money from traders. If the travellers won't pay, they are beaten and robbed. To get my pack ponies through I have to pay a great price. Be on your guard when you go that way Vennorix.'

The smith's boy nodded and Luciana, sitting at his elbow, tugged his sleeve in alarm. 'What's the Black Causeway?' she whispered. 'Is there a way round it?'

'None,' said Vennorix. 'It is a great wooden packway more than half a mile long that crosses the deep fen. The Venonii built it long ago and they charge travellers to cross it.' He shrugged. 'I have been that way many times and to be sure it is not a good place. The Venonii are warlike at the best of times and these are not the best of times. But,' and here he shrugged again, 'I doubt they will trouble themselves with small fry like us.'

At sunrise the next morning they saddled the pony and made ready for the road. Vennorix had been paid in salt for his smithing and he packed the linen sacks carefully, knowing that their value would increase the further they journeyed inland. He bid farewell to Lidda and wished him luck. 'I have sharpened all your knives,' he said. 'If the Saxon dogs come this way, show them the keenness of the blades.'

'I will,' said Lidda as he drew back the gate.

If anything, the landscape grew flatter and wetter as they travelled west. There were huge reed beds on either side of the track and the early morning sun gave way to a sullen steady rain that made the going miserable. At midday they stopped and stretched a canvas over themselves as they ate the smoked fish and bread that Lidda had given them.

'We must push on,' said Vennorix. 'We cannot risk getting to the Black Causeway after nightfall. There is a Roman villa a few miles beyond it – deserted now – like your Villa Ursini. We could make camp there. At least we would have shelter. On your feet, my slave.'

Luciana said something rude and he laughed suddenly. 'At least you look more like a native now. With your hair plastered to your head and your cloak wet and dirty, no one would take you for a Roman.'

· 6 ·

The Black Causeway

They reached the Black Causeway as the afternoon light was fading. Vennorix had grown silent as they approached it and his eyes darted around as if looking for signs of trouble. In the flat landscape it was possible to see it from a long way off. A towering structure of black wood spiked itself into the fenland sky. As they got closer, Luciana could see that it was hung with weapons and other things. She stopped suddenly as she recognised what they were. 'Skulls!' she said. 'Human skulls!'

'Just for show,' said Vennorix calmly. 'Do as I say and keep quiet. If we can't get over with a bronze coin or two, we must try silver. This is the time to open your purse, Roman girl.'

Silently, Luciana handed him a silver denarius.

A knot of men was gathered by the causeway entrance. Hunched against the driving rain, they looked ragged and famished. They were heavily armed with spears and long knives. Luciana hung back as Vennorix approached them and spent a few moments bargaining over the crossing fee. Eventually, he slapped the silver coin into the palm of one man and added to it a bag of salt from the pack-saddle. He gestured to Luciana to follow and they passed under the grim arch on to the causeway. The pony needed some persuading to step on to the wooden platform and one of the men slapped its rump. He laughed, showing a row of blackened teeth, as the pony shied in alarm.

'Softly, softly.' Vennorix tugged gently at the bridle and stepped ahead. Luciana and Ferox crept after him.

It was a planked wooden path, only inches above the fen. In places the mud oozed between the boards. It had obviously been repaired many times over the years and it was treacherously uneven and slimy. On either side the wet fen slurped and bubbled and there was a stink of marsh gas. At one point it widened out into a platform with a jetty running out into the fen. Around it, spiky wooden rails were hung with rusted blades. Luciana paused to get her breath but Vennorix urged her on.

'Not here,' he muttered. 'Evil place.'

'What?'

His voice came in a hoarse whisper. 'The priests used to come here, long ago, to sacrifice to the Unnamed One.'

'What did they sacrifice?'

'Men, so they say.'

Luciana's teeth began to chatter and it took all her concentration to keep her balance on the slimy boards. Ferox whined softly.

The causeway seemed to stretch on forever and it was with a huge sense of relief that she made out a clump of alder trees that marked the higher ground. Stepping off the black boards she dropped her pack to ease the aching in her shoulders.

'I'm glad that's over.' She glanced back and shivered.

Vennorix nodded. 'We will make for the villa up ahead and—'

His head jerked up as Ferox began to growl savagely. Luciana was aware of noises in the alder trees to her left and then a spear thudded into the ground at her feet, its shaft quivering from the force of the thrust. Vennorix whacked the pony with his stick and shouted, 'RUN!'

She ran madly, in fear of her life, hurtling down the path as if the Unnamed One was behind her. She heard the sound of the pony cantering clumsily after her and distantly she caught the noise of blade on blade and of Ferox barking and yelping. She ran until her breath gave out and then she collapsed, gasping and retching on the bank. Rigid with terror, she crouched by the path, neither daring to go onwards nor back. She started wildly as something cold and wet pressed against her arm.

'Ferox, oh Ferox!'

She hugged him frantically. He was plastered in mud and there was blood on his shoulder but he would not be quietened. Tugging at her cloak he urged her to her feet and scampered a few feet back down the path, whining and fretting. Unsteadily, she crept after him.

The pony had come to a standstill. She stroked his nose briefly before venturing on. There was no noise, the raiders seemed to have gone. But Vennorix . . . where was he?

Suddenly, she saw him. He was in the fen, chest deep and sinking.

'Help me!' His arms were outstretched on the surface of the mud feeling for something firm to grasp hold of, but there was nothing.

She lay down on the path and reached out to him. There remained an agonising gap between the tips of their fingers. For a moment she felt nothing but helpless horror, then desperation brought her quickly to her senses.

Pulling out her knife, Luciana hacked a small branch off one of the alders and laid it on the mud. Vennorix grasped it and she heaved.

The fen was reluctant to give him up and she had to fight its terrible sucking strength. But, bit by bit, he hauled himself out on to the bank and lay there gasping in a coat of black slime.

'Vennorix, are you injured?'

'A cut on my arm. Where's the pony?'

'Up the track.'

'Thieving Venonii scum, they took my gold – and your pack.'

'At least we're still alive.'

'Only just.' He stood up, spitting mud from his mouth. 'If we can make it to the villa, we might stand a chance.'

· 7 ·

The Sacrifice

They made camp in an outhouse of the deserted villa. The whole place was empty, ransacked and wrecked. She managed to light a reluctant fire against the outhouse wall and they both coughed until the smoke found its way out through the broken rafters. After unsaddling the pony she brought everything warm that she could find to wrap around the shivering Vennorix. She had already bound the knife cut on his arm with a strip of linen torn from the sleeve of her tunic but he was too muddy for her to do anything more.

They lay, exhausted, by the little fire. Ferox licked his own wound and dozed fitfully. Luciana stayed wakeful for most of the night, feeding the fire and brooding about the future. With the loss of her pack she had nothing left but the gold coins sewn into the hem of her gown. She fingered them carefully; at least they were safe.

She got up at dawn to search for more fire-wood and to check on the pony. The garden of the villa reminded her of home. It had gone to ruin but she recognised the box bushes, the rosemary and rue that had once been carefully tended. There was a bathhouse at one end of the garden. Peeping through the door she saw that the plunge pool was still full of water and that under a layer of dirt, the mosaic floor had a pattern of shells and fish. But there was a sad air of neglect about it and a dismal smell of damp plaster. Behind the bathhouse she found the remains of the villa's peat stack. The fuel was dry and she carried some of it back to stoke up her little fire.

Vennorix was awake. The caked mud had dried on him and was beginning to crack off in patches.

'We must clean your clothes,' she said to him. 'Do you have a spare tunic in your pack?'

He nodded listlessly. His face beneath the smeared mud was pale but his eyes looked fiercely bright. Fever, she thought with a pang of fear. She knew from her father that men who were injured in battle often died of wound fever. Looking at him closely she could see that he was ill.

Throughout the day she busied herself. She rigged up a trivet over the fire and cooked a pot of broth, thickening it with oatmeal and flavouring it with herbs from the villa garden. She took Vennorix's clothes and beat out most of the mud against the outhouse wall. Twice she cleaned his wound and bound it up, putting leaves of comfrey against his skin to aid the healing. Then all she could do was wait.

Ferox was limping a little but had recovered his spirits enough to go ratting. He accompanied her on a tour of the gardens while she collected more kindling wood. In a ragged meadow beyond the villa she discovered a spring of clear water bubbling up from the ground. Kneeling down and cupping her hands she took a sip from it and her tongue tingled with the icy purity of it. Idly she followed the water as it trickled along its stony bed until it was caught in a small pool surrounded by willows.

As soon as she stepped into the ring of willows she knew it was a magic place. The pool was perfectly round and the calm surface of the water reflected the sky like a mirror. On the far side, half overgrown, was a structure like a shrine and inside it stood a small statue of carved chalk. Luciana caught her breath. It was the goddess of the pool. Her outline was worn and weathered, blurred by time. Not a Roman goddess, Luciana could tell, maybe one from an older time, before even the villa was built. She shivered a little but knew that this was not an evil place, not like the platform on the Black Causeway. A shaft of sunlight fell on the water and somewhere above her head a mistle thrush began to sing in the willow branches. It felt like a place of healing. She wanted to ask for something, for a gift from the goddess, but knew that she must offer something in return.

Slowly, she rolled up her sleeve and removed the golden bracelet from her arm. For a while she sat weighing it in her palm and looking at the words, *Wear it, lucky Luciana*. Then with a swift movement she threw it into the middle of the pool. It formed a graceful arc, flashing in the sunlight before it disappeared with a faint splash into the bright water.

'Let Vennorix live,' she said softly.

She felt calm afterwards, and tired. Laying down on the bank with Ferox nestling against her, she fell into a deep sleep.

Vennorix was still burning with fever when she returned. She gave him sips of spring water and mopped his brow. As the afternoon light faded she stirred up the fire and watched the shadows leap on the outhouse walls. She sang songs to while away the time and after supper she told him a story that she had learned from Cato about the Greek hero Jason and his search for the golden fleece. Vennorix listened drowsily and smiled. Encouraged, she talked about life in the Villa Ursini, about Old Lupus and Aunt Agrippa and her cousin, little Titus. Her voice broke when she described the way she had been abandoned. Vennorix put out his hand and placed it over hers. His palm was hot and dry with fever.

'You're a brave Roman girl,' he said. 'And that's a good dog you've got; he tried to save my life. If I die, you can take my pony—' His voice trailed off and he fell asleep.

'Don't die,' she whispered urgently. 'You're my only friend.'

All night long he tossed and turned, fighting off the blankets and sometimes calling out to people in his dreams. But in the morning he was calm and when she touched his forehead, she found it cool.

'I'm hungry,' he said peevishly when he woke. 'In fact I'm starving, and my arm hurts.'

Luciana laughed. 'You've recovered your bad temper, so you must be better.'

They stayed at the villa for two more days. They both took a brief dip in the bathhouse pool then they washed their clothes and hung them over a may bush to dry.

Vennorix's wound was beginning to knit together well and he whistled as he saddled up the pony. 'What's your name Roman girl?' he asked suddenly.

'Luciana.'

'Huh, stupid name! I'll call you Luce and you can call me Venn.'

· 8 ·

The Stone Street

'What will you do if you don't find your father?'

The question had been troubling Luciana as they got closer to the Stone Street.

'I must find him,' she said grimly.

'But what if?'

There was a long pause.

'Then you will have to sell me into slavery after all.'

'Can I keep the dog?'

She gave him a shove that nearly had him in the ditch but he was laughing.

'I've still got my gear,' he said after a while. 'You were good with the bellows. I could take you on as my apprentice.'

'You mean I could be your slave.'

He kicked a stone along the track. 'No. I mean you could come to Bravonium with me – and I'd still be able to keep the dog.'

They were almost in sight of the fort now. The road was busier and Vennorix said that they would soon come to the crossing with the Stone Street. Luciana felt the rhythm of her heart begin to race. They passed another pack trader who was grazing his pony by the wayside and Vennorix stopped to greet him.

'What news, friend? Have you passed the Victrix marching down from Eburacum?'

The trader spat and shook his head. 'They're coming,' he said. 'What's left of them. I heard tell that they haven't been paid for months and they're deserting in droves. The roads won't be safe with starving legionaries abroad. And as for the rest of them, they're being stoned in every village they pass through. We must shift for ourselves now that Rome has washed its hands of us.'

Luciana fell silent but later she burst out angrily, 'It's not fair that they should be stoned; they are under orders to leave.'

'Spoken like a true Roman,' said Vennorix with a grin. 'But you must see that it leaves us undefended. We are like sheep, waiting for the wolf.'

They reached the crossroads at midday and stopped to rest for a while. Straight as an arrow, the great Stone Street sliced the landscape from north to south. To Luciana it was strangely exciting. Its surface was chalky white and rutted with the traffic of centuries. Many legions of Roman soldiers had passed that way. Now the Victrix was coming. She crossed her fingers for luck. 'Let Father be with them. Please let Father be with them.'

Beyond the massive earthen walls of the fort, the town of Durobrivae sprawled in a confusion of stinking alleys around a shabby forum. They pitched camp outside the town and Vennorix set about finding work sharpening knives and shears. It was fully a day before the cry went up.

'They're coming!'

On the horizon a great dust cloud was visible for miles and it was not long before the fore-riders of the legion clattered into the town. Grey faced and weary, they ignored the shouts of abuse from the crowd that gathered under the walls. The great oaken doors of the fort were drawn back in readiness for the legion's arrival.

Standing by the roadside, her heart thumping wildly, Luciana watched them approach. In columns of six abreast, the first century marched in, preceded by the centurion and his optio and flanked by a line of cavalry. The cornicen blew a great blast on his trumpet as the standard bearer passed into the fort. Column after column trooped after them, men haggard and grey with the dust of the road. And after them came the lumbering mule train of weapons and supplies. Hours passed as century after century marched into the fort. Finally, her straining eyes picked him out. Amongst a group of mounted staff officers, straight backed and grim mouthed, rode Marius Maximus.

A cry rose to her lips but she choked it back, feeling suddenly insignificant as the tide of the great legion swept past. She shrank back and Vennorix at her side demanded, 'Well is he there?'

'Yes,' she whispered tearfully. 'But how can I reach him? I have lost my letter of introduction from Cato.'

Later that evening, with her courage at full stretch, Luciana approached the sentry at the fort gate. With Ferox at her side and Vennorix tagging along behind, she said in faltering tones, 'I wish to speak to the legatus Marius Maximus.'

The sentry barely flicked an eyelid. 'On your way. The commander speaks to no one.'

'I assure you he will speak to me. If you tell

him that Luciana Maxima is at the gate, he will reward you for your trouble.'

'With a beating no doubt,' said the sentry but he looked her over with a careful eye.

'I am his daughter,' said Luciana, drawing herself up to her full height. 'Kindly pass on the message.'

'If this is a trick, I will flay you myself. Stand off while I speak with the optio.'

After an agonising wait, the gate creaked open and they were beckoned inside. Two legionaries accompanied them to the praetorium and stood to attention until a tall figure emerged through the doorway. Luciana stood immobile as she gazed at him. He was unshaven and his face was lined with strain but his eyes kindled with warmth at the sight of her. She felt unbearably shy.

'So, it is truly you, Luciana. How came you here?'

'I walked.'

'Old Lupus and Agrippa?'

'Gone. The villa is deserted.'

He came forward and lifted her into his arms and she wept against his shoulder.

'Hush now, we will go inside and talk. I see you still have your faithful hound. And who is this boy?'

'Vennorix. He is my . . . my friend. But for him I would not be here.'

Vennorix shuffled and looked at his feet.

Marius led them into a small lamplit guard-room and ordered wine for them. Then he sat on a bench with his hand to his brow.

'I don't have much time, Luciana. The business of the Empire presses upon me. Tell me all that has happened and then we will make plans.'

The words tumbled out and Marius listened with great attention, his mouth softening a little as she spoke of Cato's help. When she had finished he stood up and stroked her hair, then he paced about the room as he spoke.

'My days with the legion are done, Luciana. I have served my time and, officially, I am a free man. But I cannot leave my companions-in-arms at such a time. My plan was to accompany them as far as the port of Dubris, those poor devils who are willing to go, and then come back for you at the Villa Ursini. My loyalties are sadly divided; Rome has provided my livelihood but Britannia is my home. An old soldier like me can do little for the Empire now but it may be that I can defend my home. There is an old centurion of mine who is recruiting in Bravonium—'

'We know,' broke in Luciana excitedly. 'Vennorix is going to join them. He is a smith, a good one, and he wants to be an armourer. Otherwise he says we are sheep, waiting for the wolf.'

Marius smiled, giving Vennorix an appraising look. 'Then we are in agreement. Can I trust you Vennorix the smith? If I equip you for the journey, can you get my daughter safely to Bravonium?'

Vennorix grinned. 'She has saved my life once already. It is likely that she can get *me* there.'

'That is your way then, and mine too when I have seen the legion safely embarked at Dubris. Two months, maybe less, and I will join you to fight the wolf. Shall we shake hands on it?'

They did so. Tears welled in Luciana's eyes and Ferox barked.

The following day, with new sandals and fresh linen, Luciana looked westwards and sniffed the wind. 'On the road again, and my blisters not yet healed.'

Vennorix tapped the pony with his stick. 'If you travel with me, I want no complaints.'

'You shall get none, tinker, unless you are cruel to my dog.'

'It's a bargain. I would trust that dog with my life.' He whistled. 'Come boy, here boy. The open road lies ahead – and there is much wolf-hunting to be done!'

But what happened after?

They met in Bravonium and formed a company of warriors that kept the Saxons at bay for a generation. Vennorix became a famous swordsmith. Luciana married him, of course, and Ferox fathered a legion of fearless pups. No one knew what became of Old Lupus but his treasure was dug up centuries later by a farmer with a tractor and many similar Roman artefacts and coins can be seen in the British Museum in London and in many smaller provincial museums around Britain. The remains of the Villa Ursini were excavated by a team of archaeologists and no one guessed why there was a doll, a statue and a gold coin under the floor. Oh, yes, and there was a girl called Lucy who one day fished a strange gold bracelet from a pond and always felt that it was lucky.

*

Further Reading

Now you have read *The Stone Street*, you might like to read more about the Romans. Here is a selection of the many other books available.

Fiction

Rosemary Sutcliff — *Three Legions* **trilogy:**
The Eagle of the Ninth
The Silver Branch
The Lantern Bearers
Puffin Books

Non-fiction

Keith Branigan — **Roman Britain**
Reader's Digest

John D Clare — **I Was There: Roman Empire,** *Bodley Head*

Andrew Langley and Philip de Souza — **The Roman News**
Walker Books

A J Marks and G I F Tingay — **The Romans, Illustrated World History series**
Usborne

Sarah McNeill — **Roman Fort**
Tim Wood — **Roman Palace**
What Happened Here? series, *A & C Black*

Rachel Wright — **Romans, Craft Topics series,** *Franklin Watts*